llama llama

secret santa surprise

Anna Dewdney

WITHDRAWN

Based on the bestselling children's book series by Anna Dewdney

PENGUIN YOUNG READERS LICENSES
An Imprint of Penguin Random House, New York

Visit us online at www.penguinrandomhouse.com.

ISBN 9781524793623

10 9 8 7 6 5 4 3 2 1

Llama Llama and his class are practicing a song for their holiday concert tomorrow. Llama Llama plays the bell.

"Much better!" their teacher Zelda Zebra says when they finish. "If you have time to practice at home tonight, that would be grand!"

"Okay, class. It's Secret Santa time!" Zelda Zebra says.

"I'm excited . . . and nervous," Luna Giraffe says.

"Me too!" the rest of the class agrees.

"Pick one slip of paper from the hat," Zelda Zebra explains. "You get a gift for the friend whose name you picked. And do we tell anyone who it is?"

"No!" the class says. "Secret Santa is a secret!"

Everyone gets in line. When Llama Llama arrives at the front, he takes a deep breath and pulls a name from the hat. He is careful not to show it to anyone else. He has to keep it a secret.

"Can I ask you a question?"
Llama Llama asks during playtime.
"I will not tell you who my
Secret Santa is!" Euclid says.
"I just want to know what you're
looking at," Llama Llama says.
"In the sky!"
"I'm looking at clouds," Euclid
replies. "I hope they're snow clouds."

6

"Me too!" Llama Llama says. "And . . . I *do* wish I knew who my Secret Santa is."

"I wish I knew mine, too," says Nelly Gnu. "But we can't!" With that, Nelly slides down the slide.

"So, Euclid," Luna Giraffe says. "Do you think it *will* snow?"

"I hope it does," Euclid replies. "That will make the holiday perfect."

"Then we can make snow people!" says Gilroy Goat.

"And a sled train!" says Euclid. "To go down the hill in the park together!"

"That would be so great!" says Llama Llama.

After playtime, Zelda Zebra reminds the class that tomorrow is the holiday concert and gift exchange. "And until then . . ."

Everyone puts their fingers over their lips and says, "Shhhhh."

When Llama Llama sees Mama Llama, he tells her about the Secret Santa. "We have to get a gift," he says.

"Let's go to the shop," Mama Llama says.

But when they get there,
they see they are not alone!
"Mama, my whole class
is here!" Llama Llama says.
He'll have to be careful
picking out the gift.

"Oops!"

Llama Llama runs into his classmates one by one. But he walks by quickly so he won't see what they buy.

"I don't know what to get for my Secret Santa," Llama finally says.

"Just imagine your friend and think about what they usually play with," Mama says. "I'm sure they'll like whatever you end up getting them."

Llama nods and picks out a gift.

As they leave the shop, Llama and his friends see Euclid passing by on the back of his mother's bicycle.

"Everything all right?" Llama calls out to him.

"I'm on snow patrol!" Euclid replies. "There's a report of a snowflake in the park!"

That night, Llama is excited about the gift he picked out. He can't wait to get to school tomorrow.

"I hope I got the right gift," he says.

"I think you got your friend a great gift," Mama says. "It often feels even better to give a gift than to receive one. Because giving a gift makes a friend happy." Llama Llama nods and climbs into bed. Tomorrow will be the big day.

The next morning, everyone's parents come to school for the holiday party.

First, the band plays their holiday song. Llama Llama rings his bell at all the right moments.

When they finish, the parents applaud and cheer. The song sounded wonderful!

"Now, follow me," Zelda Zebra says. "It's time to open the Secret Santa gifts!"

"I'm very proud of all of you for keeping your Secret Santas secret," Zelda Zebra says.

"It wasn't easy!" Llama Llama admits. Everyone agrees.

One by one,
each classmate
gives their gift to
one of their friends.
Llama Llama hands
his gift to Gilroy,
hoping he'll like it.

Llama Llama's
Secret Santa is . . .
Luna Giraffe!
She hands him
a pink package
decorated with
a bow.

Llama Llama watches as Gilroy opens his gift—he looks happy! Then Llama Llama opens his own gift from Luna. It's a harmonica! He wants to start playing it right away.

"Thank you!" the whole class says to their Secret Santas.

Everyone had a great time picking out and opening their gifts.

Afterward, Gilroy approaches Llama Llama and says, "I really, REALLY like my gift. It's perfect!"

"You're welcome," Llama Llama replies, feeling happy. He turns to Mama Llama and says, "Now I see what you meant about giving someone a present. I wonder if this is how Santa feels!"

"Snowflakes!" Euclid suddenly calls out.

Everyone rushes to the window. He's right—real snowflakes are falling!

At the park, Euclid finally gets to lead his sled train down the hill. He was right—snow *does* make the holiday perfect. "Merry Christmas, everyone!" Llama shouts as he speeds down the hill with his friends. "Happy holidays!"